ALSO BY BILL KNOX

The Cockatoo Crime
Death Calls the Shot
Die for Big Betsy

THANE AND MOSS CASES
Deadline for a Dream
Death Department
Leave It to the Hangman
Little Drops of Blood
Sanctuary Isle
The Man in the Bottle
The Taste of Proof
The Deep Fall
Justice on the Rocks
The Tallyman
Children of the Mist
To Kill a Witch
Draw Batons!
Rally to Kill
Pilot Error
Live Bait
A Killing in Antiques
The Hanging Tree
The Crossfire Killings

WEBB CARRICK STORIES
The Scavengers
Devilweed
Blacklight
The Klondyker
Blueback
Seafire
Stormtide
Whitewater
Hellspout
Witchrock
Bombship
Bloodtide
Dead Man's Mooring

WITH EDWARD BOYD
The View from Daniel Pike

FACT
Count of Murder
Famous Trials at Glasgow High Court
Tales of Crime

ROBERT MacLEOD STORIES
Drum of Power
Cave of Bats
Lake of Fury
Isle of Dragons
Place of Mists
A Property in Cyprus
Path of Ghosts
A Killing in Malta
Nest of Vultures
A Burial in Portugal
All Other Perils
A Witchdance in Bavaria
Dragonship
A Pay-off in Switzerland
Salvage Job
An Incident in Iceland
Cargo Risk
A Problem in Prague
Mayday from Malaga